Written by
Pauline Mackay

Illustrated by
Brian Robertson

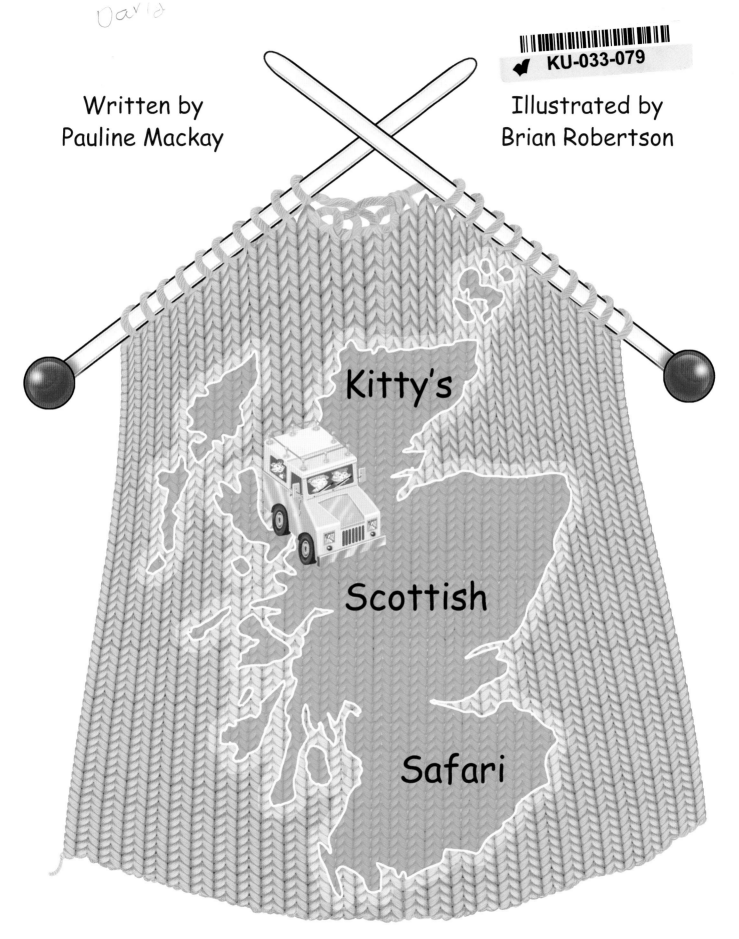

Kitty's

Scottish

Safari

Ablekids Press

Kitty Purry loves knitting, just like her Mum.

The clickety-click, clickety-click, clickety-click of Kitty's needles is a happy tune. Colourful wool dances merrily backwards and forwards – plain step, purl step, plain step, purl step – twirling and twisting into many different things.

Even on holiday, her needles are busy.

Clickety-click. 'Teko the Otter', on the Isle of Skye, has nothing to play with until Kitty makes him a yellow ball.

Clickety-click. Purple ear muffs
are a thoughtful present for
the lofty unicorn in Inverness.

"It's cold and windy up there," explains Kitty,
a little out of breath.

In Macduff, Dad takes lots of photographs
of the 'Silver Darlings'.
"How many are there?" he wonders out loud.
"This is a case for Hercule Purry."

Clickety-click. Nine blue onesies for the shiny herring.

Well done Hercule!

Well done Kitty!

Clickety ... Oh dear! Perhaps a red blanket for the bull at Alford isn't such a good idea!

Clickety-click. Warm, orange waistcoats are perfect for five playful penguins on a chilly day.
"Are we in Antarctica?" asks Hercule, with a shiver.
"No," laughs Mum, giving him a cuddle. "Today, we are in Dundee."

What a hustle and bustle in the streets of Edinburgh!
And look! Two very unusual giraffes!
Clickety-click. Kitty is pleased with their eight pink leg warmers.
"I know we aren't in Africa," pipes up Hercule confidently, "because I can't see any lions."

On exploring more of the city, however ...
Clickety-click. Kitty creates a golden
crown for the king of beasts.
"We must be in Africa now, Hercule,"
she declares mischievously.

The 'Elephant for Glasgow' is a magnificent sight. Hercule wants to examine it more closely when he learns it is made from old trains.

Clickety-click. Clickety-click. Kitty thinks her needles sound like a train on the tracks as she knits a trunk warmer in railway green.

Cli...clickety-click. Cli...clickety-click.

Nervous needles drop a stitch or two
making brown mitts in Alloway.

"That's a BIG mouse!" whispers Hercule.

Clickety-click. Clickety-click. Clickety-click.
Clickety-click. Clickety-click. Clickety-click.

Kitty is at home knitting stripy scarves for
'The Kelpies' of Falkirk. Her little paws
are going to be very tired.

Can you guess why?

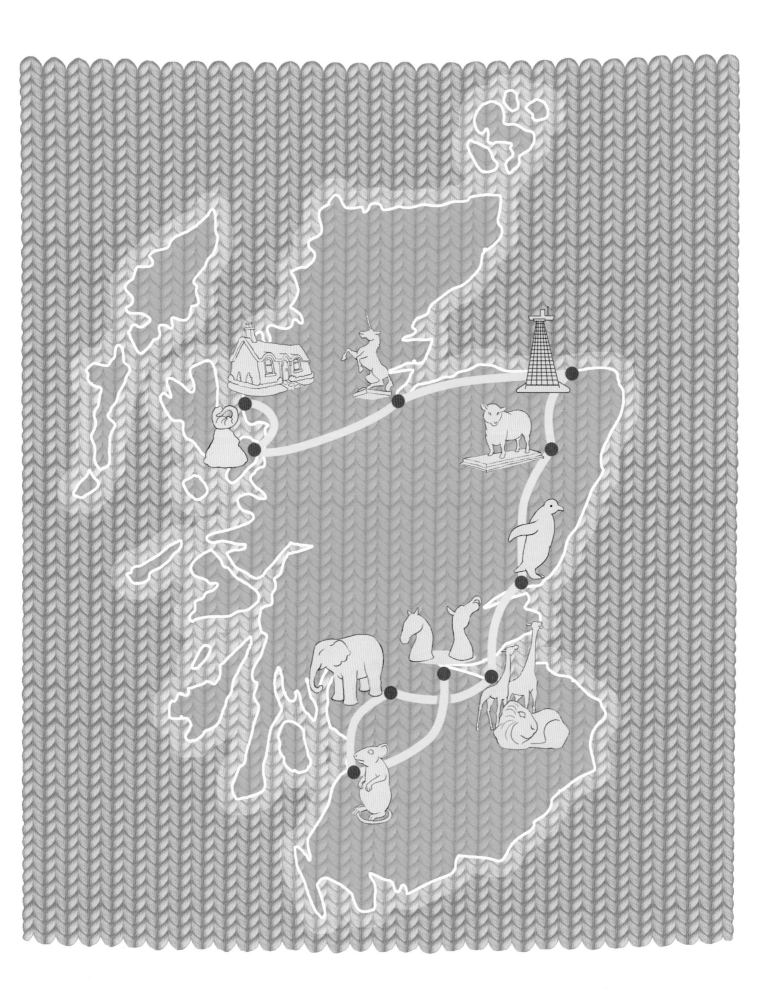

On their next trip to Edinburgh, the Purry family is going to visit 'Greyfriars Bobby'.

What animal is this?

What do you think Kitty will knit for him?

Are there any animal statues where you live?

To Anna Holsson, the inspiration for this book.   P.M.

Published by Ablekids Press Ltd
46 Ballifeary Road
Inverness
IV3 5PF
Scotland

www.ablekidspress.com

ISBN 978-1-910280-26-3

Typeset by Bassman Books
Printed in Scotland by Bell & Bain Ltd

A CIP record for this book is available from the British Library